CW00495923

BABYLON 5

THE COMING OF SHADOWS

BABYLON 5

THE COMING OF SHADOWS

THE SCRIPT BOOK OF BABYLON 5'S AWARD-WINNING EPISODE

J. MICHAEL STRACZYNSKI

WORLDWIDE PUBLISHING

BOXTREE

First published in Great Britain in 1998 by Boxtree, an imprint of Macmillan Publishers Ltd, 25 Eccleston Place, London, SW1W 9NF and Basingstoke.

Associated companies throughout the world

ISBN: 0 7522 1144 7

9 8 7 6 5 4 3 2 1

A CIP catalogue record for this book is available from the British Library

Designed and typset by Blackjacks

Printed by Mackays of Chatham plc, Chatham, Kent

Contents

Inside the House of Dreams

AN INTRODUCTION TO "THE COMING OF SHADOWS"

First, a disclaimer.

When Boxtree (through Warner Bros.) first approached me about writing a foreword to this special edition of "The Coming of Shadows," I asked what it was exactly that they wanted: my discussions with the actors about the episode, production-related stories, essays on writing...what?

Their reply: "We want you to write about what the show means to you, and what this episode in particular means to you. Most of the production-related stories have been told in the magazines, we want to get inside your head, and see what was going on when you wrote this. We're reprinting the script, not selling the episode, and we'd like to get into your brain a little."

They continued to insist on this approach even after I pointed out that what was usually going on inside my brain involved giant mutant hamsters in clown suits riding tricycles and singing old Beatles songs. Endomorphic rodents notwithstanding, they still felt that was the way to go.

As a result, this essay will be a little more personal than is usual for me...and I'm every bit as nervous about that prospect as you are, gentle reader. I can't imagine anything more tedious than a writer holding forth with, "And then I had this idea, and then, well, there was this other idea I had, and isn't this all just too brilliant of me to have figured all this out?"

Feh.

Find a magician who will tell you how he pulled that rabbit out of his sleeve, and then I'll tell you what goes on inside my brain when I write.

(...obla-dee, obla-dah, life goes on, brah....)

Sigh...day and night, it never stops.

In any event...my apologies in advance if this essay is fraught with variations on the phrase "I decided to...." They are an inevitable part of the discussion.

What follows then are my thoughts on the series, on subtext and context and What It's All Really About, and How I Got Here, and What It All Means to Me, and What I Hoped It Would All Mean to You.

Thank you.

You may sit down now.

☆ ☆ ☆

Let me start out by saying that I am scrupulously, painfully honest. It is, on balance, one of my few remaining virtues, the rest having been gradually sanded off my personality by years of exposure to Show Business and a growing suspicion that Show Business and Government Business were in reality pretty much the same thing, except that when Hollywood drops a bomb it generally doesn't flatten anyone other than the writer.

Which, I'm told, is as it should be.

But I digress.

When you only have a few virtues left, and almost no morals to speak of, you cling to those that remain with a certain desperate tenacity. There is no greater injury you can do me than to impugn my honesty or my integrity. When I give someone a promise, that person knows the promise will be kept no matter how high the price exacted in keeping it. If a clerk hands me back a dollar more in change than I had coming, I will return to the store and hand it back. If I find a wallet in the street, I will make every conceivable effort to return it, and ensure that every last credit card, dollar and nude photo of the owner's girlfriend is handed back, each in its proper place.

I am, not to put too fine a point on it, a nut about these things. So you will understand why the following aberration looms large in my conscience.

There was a time in my life when I was trying to break into television and was quite literally the prototypical Starving Artist. Emphasis on the starving. I was spending any money that came in to buy writing supplies instead of food, and at 6'4" I weighed only 150 pounds*. (Since this is being printed first in the UK, I'm sure some helpful editor will now break that down into metric in a convenient footnote.) One hot afternoon, having had virtually nothing to eat all day, I craved a candy bar. No, not craved...desired. Wanted. *Needed.* By mid-day it was all I could see. It may illuminate the desperate straits in which I found myself to consider that I couldn't even afford a candy bar.

(70 kilos)*

I began to go mad.

In that state of temporary insanity and low blood sugar – the only defense I can raise for what follows – I staggered out of the apartment, crossed the street to the corner supermarket, and shoplifted a candy bar. I barely even remember doing it. I remember only walking up the final few steps to the apartment and finding it in my hands.

Such is my capacity for instant guilt that I couldn't even eat it. I took two bites and was overwhelmed with guilt, hip deep in remorse. Jiminy Cricket was bashing my head with his umbrella and screaming obscenities that I was reasonably sure the Walt Disney company would never approve of. (I just wrote a dangling participle. I'm now feeling guilty about that as well. Do we begin to get the picture here?)

So crummy did I feel about the incident that a few days later, when I received a small check for an article I'd written for a local newspaper, I cashed the check, went to the same supermarket, purchased the same brand name candy bar, left the supermarket...then went back into the supermarket and put it back on the shelf, thereby balancing out what I'd done a few days earlier.

As I said...scrupulously, painfully, absurdly honest. So you will understand with what chagrin and utter embarrassment I now tell you the following story...which, if you will bear with me a moment longer, will explain why I am telling you all this in what is supposed to be an introduction to my script for "The Coming of Shadows."

Trust me.

I come from a working class family that was forever short on money. You'd call it lower middle class if you were being charitable, upper lower class if you were not. We moved every six months or less for years, barely staying ahead of the bills. All the while I was growing up, I assumed this was how everybody lived. I knew no better. We lived in a small apartment in the mean streets of Newark, New Jersey, with a view overlooking glass-strewn vacant lots, gangs and violence; unable to afford a refrigerator in another house, we got by during the winter by leaving the back door to one room open so the freezing air would keep the milk and other food cold; in another house ...

Again, you get the idea.

Without money to buy books, I haunted the public libraries for my dreams. Heinlein and Bradbury and Clarke and Asimov and Ellison and Lovecraft and Dunsany and Poe were my constants in a world whose longitude and latitude changed every six months. I lived for the library.

Then, for a time, I found myself living in a small town wherein the tiny, two-room library was run by an elderly woman who had a problem with a) science fiction and b) the free speech provisions of the Bill of Rights. Hence, the science fiction section consisted entirely of less than a dozen titles, almost all of them by Verne and Wells, with the occasional Bradbury thrown into the mix as a grudging nod to the latter half of the 20th century. (Except for *Fahrenheit 451*...I don't think she could tolerate that metaphor in such close proximity to her book-buying tendencies.)

So there I was: unable to afford to buy books, and without recourse at the local library.

I needed my fix of science fiction, and I wasn't getting it.

That way madness lies. Which, as noted earlier in this essay, is the only explanation I can suggest for what follows.

There was a local magazine shop that carried a fair selection of science fiction paperbacks in spinner racks alongside the comic books and the out-of-town newspapers. The owner of the shop naturally didn't encourage people to stand around reading. More than once at the beginning, when I had my nose buried in a Ted Sturgeon paperback, he would come up to me and say, "This isn't a library, you know."

My defense that the place down the street that called itself a library *also* wasn't a library didn't seem to carry much weight. I was, after all, only thirteen, and thus not yet entitled to credibility on most issues.

Finally, I had no choice (or imagined I had no choice) but to take extreme measures. Honesty and SF addiction had squared off somewhere in my Id and the latter came out the winner. I resolved to take that which I could not afford to buy.

But I would not keep it.

Picture, if you will, a young boy of thirteen slipping into a magazine store. You wait until the place gets busy, and with one quick move you sidestep between the spinner racks, where the corner mirrors can't see you, and you grab a thin paperback off the shelf. You shove it into your jacket pocket, meander out again, and make your way home hoping you don't get nailed.

Then you bring it home, and put it in a plastic baggie to keep it from getting finger prints on it during the day. At night, you pull it out from its safe haven, and *very carefully* open it just enough to read the text without breaking the spine or in any way damaging the book. You read the entire book straight through over the course of two or three nights, usually by flashlight (since you couldn't exactly explain how you got hold of a book you can't afford), then put it back into the plastic bag and press it beneath two very large mathematics textbooks that you know you will never read and would never understand even if you did read them.

At last, with the book still perfect in every way, the pages crisp and relatively untouched, you stick the book into your jacket pocket, wander back into the magazine store, and return it to the spinner racks.

This went on for months. During that time, I read the first of the New Wave SF novels, and discovered that the world was even bigger and more astounding than I had imagined.

In retrospect, I suspect that the owner of the shop knew what was going on, or figured it out in short order. I've never been particularly good at this sort of thing. Even when I haven't done anything, I have this look about me of someone who has. Every time some TV documentary runs about a convicted criminal who's escaped and is on the run...I get phone calls. So he probably knew, or at least suspected. But I was a kid, and the books were always returned in pristine condition...so he probably just looked the other way, and let me continue my education in alternate universes and distant worlds.

At least, that is the delusion with which I have salved my conscience these thirty years, and I have no intention of questioning it now.

So...why am I telling you this?

Because I had at most only a few seconds to choose which book to...borrow...from the spinner racks. I had to decide between dozens of titles, many of which were by authors unknown to me. How to tell one from the other? I had to come up with a system whereby I could instantly distinguish between the diamonds and the dross since every book that walked out with me was a possible ticket to Juvenile Hall and on balance I'd rather go up the river for a good book than a bad one, since that would only add insult to injury.

I finally determined that there was only one way to do this with any degree of consistency: I would grab the books that had emblazoned somewhere on the cover, *Winner of the Hugo Award.*

For as long as I can remember, the Hugo has embodied all that I have grown to love and respect about science fiction. It was a vote directly from the fans, the viewers, the readers, the *audience.* It was my compass leading to new writers I had never heard of before, living in small towns with names like Kankakee, Illinois, or Matawan, New Jersey, where the literary scene (if it had ever existed in the first place) shriveled up and died with Hemingway. It said to me, in the plainest terms possible, *This is important. This is noteworthy. Read this.*

And at night, beneath the covers, reading Blish by flashlight, I dreamed a thirteen-year-old's dreams of someday taking home a Hugo of my own.

Twenty-nine years later, at forty-two, I stood before an assembly of fans and media and the best and the brightest in the field of science fiction, and accepted a Hugo award for my script of "The Coming of Shadows."

You now have some notion of what that event meant to me.

☆ ☆ ☆

In true *Babylon 5* fashion, I have begun by telling you the end of the story.

Now I will tell you the beginning.

We will end somewhere around the middle.

Over the course of an average year, I appear at ten to twelve science fiction conventions, talking about *Babylon 5* and taking questions. During these Q&A sessions, sooner or later, someone – hearing of the difficulty and grief involved in bringing *Babylon 5* to life – will ask "Why did you feel you *had* to write this story?". It's one of those questions writers get, like "Where do you get your ideas?" for which there is really no good answer. (In response to this question, a number of SF writers have adopted the conceit that there is a secret business operating out of Schnectedy or White Plains, New York, which for a reasonable fee supplies all the world's writers with a fresh six-pack of ideas every three weeks. Several of these writers have since had to drop that particular fabrication after too many folks began actually believing it...which would go a long way toward proving that Darwin may have had a few of his figures plugged in backwards.)

The truest answer to the first question is, "Because I couldn't *not* write this story. Because writers, *being* writers, are sometimes taken hostage by a story that will not let go, that refuses to go away until it is told in full measure." But even that does little to illuminate the inquiry...in large measure because the inevitable follow-up question is, "Then why write it for television, where *everything* is more difficult? Why not write it as a novel or a series of novels?"

Reason 1: Because it's too damned long. Just taking my own scripts as a benchmark, since the majority of those were stories related to the five-year arc, that's seventy-one hour-long scripts (as of the end of the fourth season) plus the pilot movie plus the two TV-movies commissioned by the American TNT cable network. That's the equivalent of forty feature-film scripts in four years, or about nine full-size novels. Nine books is a *lot* of books. You can't reasonably expect your readership to wade through nine novels to get to the end of the story, and to take four or five years in the process. But in television you go into a show willing (if you like it) to stick around for, potentially, many years.

For what I wanted to do with the story, television was the more logical venue.

Reason 2: Because television is too powerful a medium, too pervasive and persuasive a form, to be left to the Visigoths and the Huns who would give us *Baywatch* round-the-clock if they thought they could make a profit on it. (And on reflection, they probably could.) Television has an obligation, a responsibility, not to make you feel better about yourself, not to preach, not to merely entertain – though at its most fundamental level it must entertain or you will never achieve anything else because no one will watch it – but also to enlighten and ennoble and uplift.

At its core, *Babylon 5* is about hope, and optimism, and our capacity to build a better world if we are willing to fight for the future, to seize it for ourselves and make of it what we want, because if we don't then someone else will make it for us, and it may not be the best possible future, or the one we most desire. It is about the nobler aspects of our humanity, those elements which call us together in common cause, not the differences that pull us apart. There are already plenty of television shows and movies and books and government programs and social agendas that have succeeded in tribalizing us, factionalizing us, marginalizing us...and not nearly enough that serve to bring us together, to reinforce that we are part of the greater community of humanity, and that in the final analysis, whatever we may have been taught to the contrary, we are more alike than we are different.

I thought, with *Babylon 5*, that I could achieve a few of these things.

Reason 3: Because a multi-year story like this, using an epic structure with a definite beginning, middle and end had never been done before on American television, even though it had been done to varying extents in the UK and elsewhere. That it had not been done before was sufficient motivation to make me want to do it.

Reason 4: Because given what would be involved in trying to achieve the goal noted in reason 3 above, I knew it would be the biggest struggle of my creative career, that I'd be banking my name and my career and my reputation on an American space-based SF series going more than three years when no such series (other than *Star Trek*) had achieved that kind of longevity in over thirty years, and that prospect scared the hell out of me.

You see, I have one major keystone in my personal philosophy, such as it is: *Find what scares you, and do it.* This scared me. As a result, if I were ever going to look at myself in the mirror again, I had to take a shot at it.

Reason 5: Because I felt it was time that there was just one television show that would look at some of the things that interest me...and if that meant I had to make it myself, then that was fine by me.

The truth is – and this will probably cause me no end of trouble out here in the land of the Lotus Eaters – I have a number of real problems with television.

The questions asked by American television dramas tend to be of the most ephemeral and trivial sort. "Will they apprehend the madman before he kills our hero?" (Yes.) "Will they find and defuse the bomb before it destroys Ms. Peachworthy's kindergarten class?" (Yes, and it's always the red wire, not the blue wire.) "Will our hero fall in love with the woman he's guarding (or vice versa)?" (Yes, and in the end she'll either turn out to be the real source of trouble, or she'll go away because guys like him don't settle down, because he's too busy being a hero...). You get the idea.

Similarly, the answers you get from most such television shows are equally ephemeral. An answer is only as good as the question; you can only get pertinent information by asking impertinent questions, but as a result of the influence of pressure groups, religious zealots, censors and governmental agencies, most television shows have been sufficiently defanged that they tend to shy away from impertinence, real or perceived.

Too many easy answers, and not damned near enough good questions.

I wanted to do a show that would ask some of those questions.

Consider, for example, the *Babylon 5* episode "Passing Through Gethsemane." Here we have the story of a monk, a man of God, dedicated to serving humanity, a good and kind and decent man who discovers to his horror that in the past he had been a serial killer...a murderer who was apprehended, convicted, and sentenced to the death of personality: his memories were erased, and his personality wiped, replaced with a manufactured personality propelled by the desire to serve the community harmed by his actions.

What is the disposition of this man's soul? Is his soul the soul of a good man, or a murderer? Which is the *real* person? How does he face his God knowing what he has done? How does he do penance, how does he ask forgiveness for crimes he does not remember committing? What is the nature of forgiveness and punishment? Where does justice end and revenge begin? How can we as people forgive him, and the others like him?

The questions asked in that episode are not the sort of questions usually asked in American television. But they are precisely the sort of questions I wanted to investigate.

(Note: I say "usually" above because it is not my intent that this foreword give either *Babylon 5* or myself by implication undue credit. There are a number of other television writer/producers striving to create intelligent, well-considered and thoughtful dramas. Very few of them make it to the small screen, but when they do we are all enriched by their presence. My comments here are directed at the majority of television programs, not the few who manage to somehow dance past the gun towers and the guard dogs to provide a richer level of entertainment.)

I'm often asked by reporters what quality most attracts our viewers, and I think it is that aspect, that there is a hunger for real discussion, for real meat among the cotton candy, for someone to talk about who we are, and where we're going...and to talk about the future, because nobody else seems to be doing it.

I wanted to do a show that would consider *process* and *change*, in a medium where no matter what happens during the course of an episode, the series is reset back to zero by the end of the hour. And I wanted to do this on both the small scale, and the large.

In most science fiction television, from the very first episode on you know who the players are: the bad guy, the good guy, the comic relief, the love interest...they are all spelled out from the first frame, and remain locked into those positions for the duration of the series. Their relationships, and the relationship of one government or force to another, may momentarily alter as required by the need to keep the story fresh, but the characters and situations are fundamentally set in stone.

Now consider Londo in the first season. A figure sometimes comic, sometimes tragic, but powerless in either configuration. A patriot who dreams of the past and desires it for his future because his present is a burden to his soul and his dignity. He has seen the Centauri Republic decline, diminish, grow soft and somnolent. He wishes to wake it to greatness once more because he so identifies with his Republic that unless it is great, he cannot be great...and, contrariwise, the Republic may never become great until he can become great, and personally lead it into the future he envisions. And in that respect he is correct; the fortunes of the two are linked, which in the final analysis is key to Londo's tragic arc.

He begins as buffoon and comic relief, with some tragic elements, and over the course of the story grows to become prime minister and then emperor, acquiring greater power and even greater burdens along the way until at the last he surrenders them with fatigue, ready to make an end of it because he can no longer bear the weight of his own continued existence. As I told actor Peter Jurasik when first explaining Londo Mollari, "He goes from comic and tragic, to comic and dark, to tragic and dark, and then at the end to tragic and light." We see all his changes, all his colors, over the course of the story.

And we see that Londo falls not because he failed, but because he got exactly what he wanted, just not in the way he wanted it.

Similarly, I went to great lengths to make audiences assume that G'Kar was the Bad Guy...and thus began the long road toward making him something far greater: a hero of sorts, a religious figure who learned that there are other ways to solve a problem than the violence that had been the hallmark of his life before arriving at Babylon 5. His character travels an arc leading from villainous manipulator through a series of transformational incidents to become a true leader: trusted, wise and in his curious way, even kind.

Delenn undergoes the most visually dramatic and literal transformation, going from pure Minbari to a physical bridge between the Minbari and Human species. We see her begin to acquire human habits and emotional traits, and begin to apply more human solutions (individuality, spontaneity) to the problems that confront her. The story charts her progression from simple acolyte to the chosen disciple of Dukhat, a member of the Grey Council, an ambassador with a secret agenda, a lover for Sheridan, a leader of the Rangers, and finally the leader in partnership with Sheridan of a new Interstellar Alliance.

Sheridan goes from a well-regarded straightforward soldier to a reluctant diplomat, to rebelling against his own government, dying and returning, and becoming leader with Delenn of the ISA...Vir grows from Londo's (seemingly) spineless assistant to a mature character who fights for what he believes in, and eventually becomes emperor himself...Lennier grows from a naive acolyte who could barely bring himself to look up at Delenn to her valued companion and advisor, trained to follow in her footsteps, along the way acquiring wisdom and strength enough to defend her with his own life if necessary...Franklin, Ivanova, Sinclair, Garibaldi, Zack, Lyta, even Kosh, all undergo transformations or change along the course of the story to become something more than they were when they arrived.

Similarly, in most television science fiction, all the major forces are in play and established right from the start. By contrast, I wanted to examine how governments rise and fall through incidents of war and changes in the disposition of their leaders. In any other show, a group like the Nightwatch would have been in place from the beginning. More important to me was the opportunity to track the development of such an organization, from a small division of a new ministry, to its methods of recruitment by money and prestige and an open appeal to the better natures of the citizenry on points that seem reasonable at first glance... to less reasonable positions, more extreme actions, until it became the fist used to repress the very society it once claimed to serve. To track the birth and death of a fascistic organization would be entertaining on the one hand, and illuminating on the other...perhaps even useful in evaluating the future growth of such groups in the real world.

Because it's dangerously easy to point to Nazi Germany or Stalinist Russia and say, "Oh, well, that could never happen *here*." Well, in fact, it *can* happen here, the only difference being the amount of time that has passed wherever your own "here" happens to be since prosperity has fled, since despair has taken root, since scapegoats were named and identified, since national pride became national paranoia. Wherever your particular "here" happens to be, at some point or other, it *has* happened here, and it *will* happen here again...unless we are very wise and very careful; unless we make it a point to remember how these things get started. Hence the Nightwatch.

Another part of the process that I wanted to examine was the way we move from peacetime to war and back again: the justification of war, the preparations for war, the fighting of a war, the winning (or losing) of a war, and just as importantly, the aftermath of war. Because fighting a war is easy; making the peace, that's hard. Blowing up a home, a nursery, a bank or a church takes less than five seconds. Rebuilding them can take months or even years.

Rebuilding souls takes considerably longer.

A common saying in Britain during World War II was, "The duration's gonna last a lot longer than the war." And it's the duration that fascinates me. War is a litany of bomb blasts and body counts, photos of brave young men and women who laid down their lives for a cause, a country, a belief, a crusade, all of it coming so fast that we barely have time to consider it all. In peace time, there is too much time to consider it all, and that's when the price is most truly paid by those left behind, who can best honor the dead by continuing on, pushing ahead, and remembering the names of those who will not be coming home as we build the next sequence of tomorrows, hoping always that the last big war will *be* the last big war.

Humans survive.

It's what we *do.*

Sometimes, though, it just hurts like a sonofabitch.

But that's where the drama is. That's where the story is. That's where the heart is. I know this also because in my entire life, I have seen only one photograph that made me cry. Not cry as in a few tears, or weeping...I mean wracking, sobbing, shuddering, *crying.* I was reading through one of our national news weeklies and stumbled across the photo of a young woman beside the grave of her husband, a soldier killed in action. The sky was a perfect blue, and she was sitting on the grass, her arms around the tombstone, face resting on the edge of the cold stone, just as she would have wrapped her arms around her husband's shoulders. But he wasn't there. Only the stone remained.

I defy you to conjure up that image in your head, to *really* see it ... and not weep.

And I thought, if in this story I can make you feel even a fraction of the raw emotion that picture contained, the statements it made about the folly of war and the strength of those who are left behind to endure, then I will have accomplished something of value with my life.

I hope that I've done that. But only time will tell, and when that decision is made, I will likely be long turned to dust.

But it's worth the effort to try.

Back to the point:

I wanted to make a show that was, or at least felt unpredictable, while at the same time putting some of my cards on the table for all to see, in advance of the actual event. In many cases, we are shown a glimpse of *Babylon 5*'s future: Londo and G'Kar strangling one another, Vir becoming emperor, Sheridan having married Delenn and fathering their child. You see the end of the story, or a part of the end. I tell you exactly what I'm going to do, that I'm coming right up the middle at you...but you won't know what or when or how or where, and sometimes the viewer discovers that what *looked* one way, was actually something utterly other. Because again it's all about *process*, about how we get from point A to point B.

One could say, of *Moby Dick*, "At the end, Ahab and the whale disappear into the sea." That is the resolution of it. But the story is the process of getting there.

Someone once pointed out the difference between incident and story. Incident is, "The King died and then the Queen died." Story is, "The King died and then the Queen died of grief."

Everything is context and subtext. The *how* and the *why*, not the what.

Which is why Morden arrives to ask "What do you want?" The darker side of our intellect strives for the *thing*, the goal, to have, to acquire, to own. It is the Id unbridled. The Vorlons ask "Who are you?" Who is it that is doing the wanting? How do you know what you want until you know who you are? Once again, *process* vs. *goal*.

Answering "What do you want?" before you know who you are will almost always lead to a self-destructive answer. On the other hand, to answer "Who are you?" before deciding what it is that you want will almost always lead to a more positive answer.

Then, of course, there is Lorien's question: "Why are you here?" And that's the big one. That's the puzzler, the one question that cannot be definitively answered this side of the grave, so we have to come up with our own version of the answer.

Process. *Babylon 5* is and has always been about process. About going from *here* to *there*, emotionally, physically, as members of society and children of Earth.

And process is sometimes unpredictable. So I wanted there to be moments in the series in which the viewer would come away unsettled ... moments during an episode when the viewer would come to the uncomfortable conclusion that either there was no one at the wheel, or there was a madman at the wheel, but either way the car was out of control and therefore *anything* could happen.

Finally, I wanted to create a show that would address three fundamental issues: choice, consequence, and responsibility.

It is in the vested interests of any society, any form of government, any hierarchical system to make you believe that you have no power, that you have no choices, that you cannot fight City Hall or Parliament or the Party or the Committee. We are told to play nice, to behave, to get along, that the human being singular can't really change anything, can't affect anything. Leave it to the rest, to the authorities, to those qualified to deal with the problem. They want you to go to sleep, to believe that there is nothing you can do.

They are, of course, quite wrong. And when they tell you you cannot do anything, that you do not have a choice, they are lying to you. Nothing more, nothing less.

History was changed by one assassin in Sarajevo, whose bullet set off a chain reaction that led to World War I and by default to World War II and much of the Cold War history thereafter. American history was changed by another man with another bullet at a book depository in Dallas; in President Lincoln's private box inside Ford's Theater in Washington DC; in the Ambassador Hotel in Los Angeles; outside a hotel, an office building, a New York brownstone when John Lennon signed the wrong fan's album cover.

One man with a bullet can change the world. We've seen it. We know it's true.

How much more can one man or one woman with one idea change the world? Ask Mahatma Ghandi, Mother

Theresa, John Kennedy, Nelson Mandela, Benjamin Franklin, Thomas Aquinas.

And while you're at it...ask yourself.

Babylon 5 tells us that we have choices, that we can go left or right, and that we must consider why we choose and where we want to go. It tells us that we are not powerless. This is not exactly a revelation; but it sometimes helps to say these things out in the open.

Babylon 5 also tells us that these choices have consequences for the world and the people around us. We do not operate in a vacuum. If we strike a blow, someone will bleed; if we start a war, someone will die; if we build a home, someone will live in it; and if we extend our heart, someone will eventually embrace it.

Finally, it tells us that we must assume responsibility for our choices and their inevitable consequences. And that's the hard one, the one that operates in contradiction to the common notion of Every Man for Himself, Sod the Other Guy, It's Not My Fault, Shit Happens and other assorted bumper stickers.

When I was first trying to sell *Babylon 5*, a studio exec said, "Okay, let's cut to the chase, what's the story really about, I mean, *really* about?"

I considered it for a moment, and foolishly decided to tell him the truth. "Choices, consequences and responsibility."

He mulled it over for a moment. "Okay, but who's the bad guy?"

"We are."

"Uh, huh. And who's the good guy?"

"We are."

Suffice to say the meeting went downhill from there.

But the funny thing is, see, it ain't about meetings.

It's about the gentleman at a convention in Texas who said he was sufficiently moved by these three notions that he changed his major from business to social work, and is now helping others to find their own way through the darkness...it's about the couple in Chicago who felt trapped in jobs they did not want, a life they did not choose, who through the show realized finally that they do have a choice, and struck out on their own, no money, no job offers, and crossed half the United States to the place where they had always wanted to live, to find the jobs they always wanted to have...because they *chose* to do so.

I have many friends on the East Coast of the US who constantly complain about the weather, the crime, the neighborhood, the conditions, the lack of jobs. They hate it, they say.

"So move," I say.

"Well, we can't, we don't know anybody outside the area, at least we know we've got something here even if we hate it, so what're we gonna do?"

"Go," I tell them. "Just ... *go*."

They don't. They'll continue to find reasons to stay where they don't want to stay, and do what they don't want to do, because it is easier than risking, than doing, than choosing.

Let me tell you about elephants.

(I know, I know...you're wondering what the hell this sermonette has to do with "The Coming of Shadows." It has everything to do with it. Stick with me, we're almost there.)

If you've ever been to the circus, you'll notice that the younger elephants wear big huge manacles attached to big huge chains tied to big huge spikes sunk four feet into the ground... but the larger elephants, the older ones, have very thin ropes tied around one foot attached to a spike maybe a foot or so into the ground.

Why the difference? Why the contradiction? Would the larger elephant not need a much heavier chain than the younger one?

No...because of a little psychological trick called *conditioned helplessness.* As a young elephant, it cannot move, cannot escape, because the chain is too heavy and solid for it to get away. Over time, the elephant gets used to the idea that whenever it feels something on its leg, it is tied to something too powerful to break and thus it cannot escape...even though in reality it could snap those bonds very easily.

When our world and our choices are restricted over a sufficiently long period of time, we come to believe that we cannot snap our bonds, cannot choose anything other than what we have, even though those bonds are often as sheer as gossamer.

And it's when we are in that state of conditioned helplessness that we are truly at our most dangerous, to ourselves as we fall into despair or poor decisions, and to others when the weight of the perceived chain becomes too much, and like enraged elephants we go mad...and make those around us pay the price for our confinement.

☆ ☆ ☆

I have told you all this, explained all this, because *Babylon 5* as a whole incorporates all of the goals I wanted to achieve, and of all the episodes produced, "The Coming of Shadows" is the one episode most emblematic of the themes I wanted to communicate. They are all here, writ large or small.

The story begins with G'Kar raging at Sheridan at the forthcoming arrival of Centauri Emperor Turhan (only named subsequent to the episode after the actor who brought the role to life, Turhan Bey). Here we get a taste of the first season G'Kar in all his splendor, still awaiting transformation here in the second season: raging, upset, intemperate, scheming to personally kill Turhan in retribution for past outrages perpetrated against the Narns. "Don't do something we'll both regret," Sheridan cautions him. "It's too late for that," G'Kar replies, when in fact it is not too late. But G'Kar's mind is already made up, so he refuses to acknowledge that he does have a choice.

And that choice is to listen to Sheridan's warning and at least listen to what Turhan has to say, find out *why* he is coming...or to take action without having all the facts. Because he has refused to consider even the possibility of the former, G'Kar defaults to the latter path, believing that if Turhan comes to Babylon 5 then he must strike the Emperor down. Cause and effect, not rational decision-making. He allows himself to be controlled by the past. Thus he begins to prepare for the planned assassination, putting his affairs in order.

In contrast to his earlier scene with Sheridan here G'Kar is calm, peaceful...almost happy. "The path is clear," he says. There is no longer indecision, which causes inner conflict and stress. But it is a false calm, based on taking the easy way, rather than the considered way. If he believes he has no choice, then he cannot possibly be conflicted or confused.

Turhan, on the other hand, *is* aware of his choices. He can stay on Centauri Prime, where it is safe, but instead chooses another way: to go to Babylon 5, even knowing the risk to his health, in the hope of achieving a greater purpose. It is a knowledge he has come to late in life; we later hear him lament that in the course of his life, he never chose much of anything: his role was thrust upon him and he has done the best he could to live up to that role. "It never occurred to me to choose otherwise," he says. Only now, toward the end of his life, does he understand that he must now make a choice.

Even his dialogue when he first arrives at the station is emblematic of this. He is moved that Sheridan and the others would choose to be here, to remain in harm's way. In his private meeting with Sheridan, he asks if Sheridan chose to join Earthforce or if he was conscripted. Sheridan's reply, that he wanted to be a part of something that was greater than himself, reflects Turhan's own purpose in coming to Babylon 5: to achieve something more, to create the greater good.

"The past tempts us, the present confuses us, and the future frightens us, and our lives slip away, moment by moment, lost in that vast, terrible in-between." The in-between is the failure to choose, caught between three forces (past, present, future) like a horse caught between two bales of hay, unable to decide which way to go, and thus going nowhere. He has chosen (again that word) to step outside the paralysis paradigm, to do something, even at the possible cost of his own life.

When Turhan is struck down by illness brought on by his choice, it's Londo who is propelled to move into the spotlight by his own sense of personal destiny and the knowledge that others are moving into position back home to take advantage of the situation. He will invoke the Shadows to retake a base in Quadrant 14.

Here his decision is much like G'Kar's, illuminating how much these two characters are alike in some ways, and how they are linked at the hip. G'Kar believes that he must act in a certain way due to what has been done to his people in the past; here Londo believes that he must act because of what he wants for his people in the future. Under normal circumstances, Londo would never have called for an attack of this magnitude; but the current circumstances are anything but normal, and to Londo they not only justify the action, they *require* the action, just as G'Kar believes that the circumstances *require* his own response.

"I have no choice," Londo says.

"Yes, you do!" Vir tries to tell him, to no avail. "Once you start down this road, there's no going back." And again he is correct. Vir, who has never before stood in Londo's way, now steps forth and is not only forceful, he is tragically accurate. Like G'Kar, Londo has not thought through the long-term implications of his actions; he is thinking only of the moment.

Now comes a very important transitional moment in G'Kar's life. He is on a cusp; until this moment, G'Kar has considered his people to be on the rise, aggressive, giving back to the Centauri what he believes they deserve. Sometimes swaggering, usually manipulative, cocky and self-assured, he is about to have the pins knocked out from under him in a way that will cause him to reconsider his life and his approach in coming stories.

The scene begins with the last we will see of the first season G'Kar...at his best when planning to get someone, almost furious with the universe that his assassination has been thwarted by the emperor's imminent death by natural causes. "Never in my life have I seen a case of worse timing!" His dialogue here is deliberately dark-comic: "All they have to do is prop him up for a few minutes."

Then comes the unexpected: his discovery that Turhan had come with the express purpose of apologizing. The very idea was incomprehensible to him because he never stopped to consider that anyone might feel that way. "And maybe that's the biggest tragedy in the damned story," Franklin says, a slight but forgivable bit of auctorial intrusion.

And the scales fall from G'Kar's eyes, and he is suddenly, abruptly awakened to another world: a world of *choices.* He does not have to be bound by the past, does not have to be tied to hatred, does not have to be confined to the laws of action and reaction...like Turhan, he can *choose* to step outside the familiar patterns and effect change.

That realization changes G'Kar. It also sets in place the foundation to make his subsequent betrayal all the more painful.

In a bit of parallel construction, while G'Kar is having a revelation about the past, Londo is having a revelation about the future...again subliminally reinforcing the elements to which they are both unwitting prisoners.

In his dream, Londo achieves his goal, and becomes Emperor. But he is old, and sick, and something is very much wrong. We see G'Kar appear in the room, one eye missing, and continue to watch as he and Londo strangle one another to death. Here is an example of a case where I put my cards on the table: I showed the viewer one of the ends of the story. Not a false future, but a real one. Many fans of the show suggested that they didn't find the situation believable because how could G'Kar slip into what would almost certainly be a well-guarded room like that to attack Londo?

In making this assumption, they did not allow for other possibilities. As with G'Kar, they worked from the image of the past to construct an unchanging future. They saw *what* had happened, but not the *why* or the *how*...which, as revealed later, showed us a Londo very different than he is at this point in the story: a prisoner to a shadow-creature called a Keeper, who controlled his actions. A Keeper who was temporarily disabled through Londo's excessive drink, letting him be himself again just long enough to free an imprisoned Sheridan and Delenn, then ask G'Kar to end his life, thereby finally freeing him from the Keeper and the horror that had become his life.

That G'Kar's act could be one of mercy, at Londo's request, was something that was unpredictable at this point in the story, but which makes absolute consistent sense once you understand what happened between *now* and *then.*

Unpredictable but consistent...again, one of my goals with the show.

We see that Londo will become emperor, but not how; we see that Shadow vessels will come to Centauri Prime, but not how. Again, the use of foreshadowing, which is not a typical device in American television on this scale. (Those ships would not come to Centauri Prime until the next season.) The image of a hand reaching out of a red star is a reflection, for those who were on board, to "The Geometry of Shadows," where Elric the technomage tells Londo, "I see a great hand reaching out of the stars...the hand is your hand."

According to television logic, this plan of Londo's to attack the colony in Quadrant 14 and start a war between the two races would somehow be thwarted at the last moment. We wait for something to intercede, a spatial anomaly that prevents the ships from arriving at their target, allowing time for a solution to the problem to be found. But like a nightmare that is out of control (hence, again, Londo's dream sequence), the attack comes.

We see Londo's choice, the cost of that choice and in very short order...its consequences.

Now we come to my favorite scene in the script: Londo and G'Kar in the Zocalo. We know the attack has just occurred, so when we first see G'Kar coming at Londo, we suspect the worst, as does Londo. Then the terrible realization: even as Londo tries to get away, we see that G'Kar has changed, if only a little; he is willing to follow up on the example of the Emperor, and set the past aside in the hope of building a better future.

He extends Londo the hand of peace...something that would have been impossible for him even to imagine. A goal that might even potentially be more important than recovering Quadrant 14, but that is not foremost in Londo's mind as he sits across from a G'Kar who actually drinks a toast to the

Emperor's health. We, the audience, know what Londo has done, even if G'Kar does not (yet), and we recognize the emotions behind Londo's eyes: regret, pain, remorse, sadness...a sense of a missed opportunity, a chance that will almost certainly never come again.

Londo recognizes here that he did have a choice, and the heavy cost that will come from his decision. He has betrayed G'Kar, and G'Kar doesn't even know it yet...which makes his pain even that much greater.

This, and the following encounter between Centauri and Narn forces further serves to give the sense that the episode is out of control, that all the things we expect of a television show, to somehow avoid a conflagration on this scale, have not happened. Londo and G'Kar have had their reasoned discussion, but too late to change anything. Events are spinning out of control, and will only escalate further.

The deaths that come through all this are the direct consequence of Londo's choice, made in a foolhardy moment for personal gain; the death of Prime Minister Malachi is also a direct consequence of this, even though Londo was not personally involved and may not have had advance knowledge of it; and of course the war itself springs from this choice. The consequences now weigh most heavily on his shoulders, and over the next several years he will continue to deny his responsibility for this, which only leads to further mistakes in future, such as the bombing of the Narn homeworld in "The Fall of Night."

Next we see G'Kar's rage as he discovers that he has been betrayed. For most of the first season and the second season to date, we have been waiting for someone to kick G'Kar where it hurts, to make up for some of the things he has done...but now, for only the second time in the show (once before, in a smaller fashion, preparing the way for this episode, in "By Any Means Necessary") we feel great sympathy for G'Kar. His position in our eyes changes instantly. We have all been betrayed by someone at some point in our lives, and we can immediately identify with his feelings of pain and frustration and need for revenge.

And when he attempts to go to Londo, and breaks down before Sheridan – knowing that retribution will only bring greater death to his people – G'Kar's transformation is complete, from manipulator to tragic/heroic figure, sacrificing his pride and his revenge for the good of his people...and Londo, whom we have seen as variously comic or friendly or at least benign, takes on the full aspect of a monster for the first time.

"Leave him alone," Sheridan says, his sadness and pity, his desire to protect the wounded G'Kar transferring to the audience, "leave him alone." And at that moment, G'Kar is utterly and completely alone, in a place where no one can touch him and no one can help him.

In that instant, for Londo and G'Kar, their roles are reversed. Another stated goal of the show.

In another bit of foreshadowing, the Emperor asks Kosh, "How will this end?"

"In fire," the Vorlon tells him. And, of course, we see many interpretations of this: Centauri Prime in ashes, the Narn homeworld bombed, and the final end of the Shadow War in the episode "Into the Fire."

Even after all this, Londo has one more chance to set things right. He could repeat the truth of what the dying Emperor tells him with his final breath. Instead, he chooses to lie, to protect himself and Refa and the plans they have set in motion. "You are both doomed," Turhan told Londo...a price which Refa considers small enough in exchange for immortality.

Again, both characters (Refa and Londo) are tied to the future, willing to sacrifice the present in any of its forms to create a particular future...even at risk of damnation.

These themes, as seen here, and voiced by Turhan, permeate this episode and the series in general: the needs of the future vs. the sins of the past, and the delicate balance point that we must find between them or risk sacrificing the present.

Then, finally, the last movement of the episode: G'Kar's declaration of war. This moves the show forward on a definite arc, and changes the nature of the show from a cold-war "let's try and avoid violence" stance to a war-time position which continues for some time.

In this way, we map how a war may begin...in the acts of one man, who chooses wrongly, and sets things in motion that soon spin out of his control. Wars are sometimes planned, and they are sometimes blundered into. Here was a case of the latter. We have followed the tensions between Narns and Centauri from the very first episode (in which we also first learned of Londo's dream), track the many points along the way where this war could have been avoided, segue into the war proper, and then the incidents during and after the surrender by the Narn government.

This allows *Babylon 5* to be not just a story about a war, but rather the history of a war, the events before, during and after. At its best, *Babylon 5* speaks with the voice of future history, and with "The Coming of Shadows" that voice rises to a shout.

It is the linchpin in the first two years of the series, the one that most conclusively points to the fact that this is a story with a definite beginning, middle and end; that the characters will change and evolve; that plots the course of a war through all its various stages; that works against the notion of a clearly defined good guy and a clearly defined bad guy; and shows the dangers of conditioned helplessness, in which we believe all our decisions of the future must be based on outside factors, that we have no real control over our lives, our decisions, or our future.

It is, quite simply, the quintessential *Babylon 5* episode.

☆ ☆ ☆

It's a strange feeling, sitting here and typing these words, at this particular moment. We have come a long way from "The Coming of Shadows," through the Shadow war, the civil wars on Earth and Minbar, the secession of Mars and other colonies, and the birth of a new Alliance. The story has blossomed out, and so has the series itself.

When we first went on the air, the critics panned *Babylon 5* and said we wouldn't last a season. They said that the only decent SF being done today could be found on *Star Trek* and that we were a poor pretender to the throne. Many in the fan community took the same position, and several of us involved with *Babylon 5* found ourselves being booed at conventions for even presuming to create a show in a genre that had been all but conceded to *Star Trek*.

Because of the vagaries of American syndicated television, we were barely a blip on the radar screens: very few people even knew we existed. Like the Babylon 5 station itself, the odds were stacked against us in a universe that was either benignly neglectful or downright hostile to our intentions. Nobody thought we'd make it...and with cause, since no American space-based future SF series other than *Trek* in its various incarnations has survived this long in 30 years.

But survive we did, through one season, then two, then three, and now four, with news of a fifth season confirmed even as I write these words. Our cast members are now valued guests at conventions; we are now being broadcast in virtually every major country around the world; many critics have come around to applaud *Babylon 5* as something new and innovative and challenging; awards have begun showing up in our offices at increasingly frequent intervals....

And now, "The Coming of Shadows," the pivot episode in which we first showed what we could really do when we put our minds to it, is given the honor of this publication.

And best of all, it has the words "Hugo Award Winner" on the cover. What goes around, comes around.

You'd think that would be enough.

And it almost is.

There's just one more thing.

This book would be incomplete if I did not take the time to acknowledge openly the gratitude of myself and everyone involved with *Babylon 5* to every member of the B5 fan community, because without their support and help and encouragement when we were virtually a stealth television program, I doubt if we could have resisted the urge to simply go mad and give up. And we most certainly would not be on the air; their (your) letter-writing campaigns, phone calls, viewing parties, conventions and room parties have helped to forge a new community of fans, many new to science fiction, who help each other, support one another and the show itself.

I hear, regularly, from fans who announce on the net that they are going to be showing a copy of a new B5 episode fresh off the satellite, and invite strangers to their home to watch the show with them...who gather in pizza parlors and restaurants to watch the show together and break into discussion groups later to analyze the themes we've chosen to explore that week...I hear from the nuns in the Chicago convent who watch our show...from those in the military in Bosnia and Korea and elsewhere for whom the show is a morale booster sent on tape to air bases and carrier groups and ground units...from the University of York in the UK which will host an academic conference on the themes of *Babylon 5* this winter...from students and rabbis and whole families where the show has bridged three generations who watch the show together...from those who have committed their own time to building web pages and internet sites and news groups so that others can catch up with the show....

I hear about all of that, and more...and there are no words in this language or any other for the intense, profound gratitude that I and everyone else involved with *Babylon 5* feel toward those who have volunteered their energies in the battle to keep this show on the air, and to embrace other fans around the world. They have taken *Babylon 5*'s example and formed communities of divergent voices raised in common cause.

That community of B5 fans has been the one unexpected development...and on balance perhaps the most rewarding. If this show is truly about choices, consequences and responsibility, then it was the fans who chose to support us, with the consequence that we are still on the air as I write this, and the responsibility for that...is yours.

Thank you.

☆ ☆ ☆

As you turn now to the script itself, I hope that you will find it an interesting exercise to run the episode in the background and compare the script, shot for shot, with the actual finished episode. You will find some bonuses along the way here, bits of dialogue and scenes omitted from the final cut when we ran long. What was cut, and why, should be illuminating.

My final thanks I reserve for those who have been closest to my heart and my vision during the years of creating *Babylon 5*: my partner, Doug Netter; line producer John Copeland, without whom this show would never get made; producer George Johnsen, without whom this show would not look and sound and be as good as it is; and the most talented assembly of cast, crew and support staff it has ever been my pleasure to work with.

Because the words are meaningless without actors to give them voice, carpenters to build the sets, painters to paint them, costumers to dress the cast, computer EFX to dazzle the eye, and a host of other technicians and stage wizards.

Without them, "The Coming of Shadows" would have been one man sitting on a chair, reading the script aloud. Probably me.

And if that prospect doesn't frighten you, let me state emphatically that it scares the hell out of me.

So regards from *Babylon 5*, gentle reader; I hope that you will find the following enlightening or at least instructive, and wish you the best of luck in following your own path through the house of dreams.

Just remember...that first step is a doozy.

J. Michael Straczynski

28 May 1997

Sherman Oaks, California

The Coming of Shadows

CAST

CHARACTER	**ACTOR**
SHERIDAN	BRUCE BOXLEITNER
IVANOVA	CLAUDIA CHRISTIAN
GARIBALDI	JERRY DOYLE
DELENN	MIRA FURLAN
G'KAR	ANDREAS KATSULAS
LONDO	PETER JURASIK
DR.FRANKLIN	RICHARD BIGGS
VIR	STEPHEN FURST
REFA	WILLIAM FORWARD
CENTAURI EMPEROR	TURHAN BEY
CENTAURI PRIME MINISTER	MALACHI THRONE
CUSTOMS GUARD (#1)	BRYAN MICHAEL McGUIRE
RANGER	REDRIC LEHNE
KHA'MAK (NARN)	NEIL BRADLEY
NARN PILOT #1	KIM STRAUSS
NARN PILOT #2	JONATHAN CHAPMAN
ZACK ALLAN	JEFF CONAWAY

POST

VOICE OF KOSH	ARDWRIGHT CHAMBERLAIN

WRITTEN BY J. MICHAEL STRACZYNSKI

SETS

INTERIOR

Centauri

- Centauri Palace Grand Chamber

Babylon 5

- Sheridan's Office
- Customs Area
- Londo's Quarters
- Downbelow
- Docking Bay (CGI)
- G'Kar's Quarters
- Blue Corridor
- Sanctuary
- Central Corridor
- Garden/Rotunda (CGI/Composite)
- Rotunda
- Crew Corridor
- Medlab/Hallway Between Infirmary & Medlab
- Narn Fighter
- Zocalo
- Narn Fighter
- Garibaldi's Office
- Observation Dome
- Green Sector Hallway
- Council Chambers
- Delenn's Quarters

EXTERIOR

Space

- Near Centauri Palace
- Centauri Capital
- Jumpgate
- Centauri Prime
- Planetside
- Narn City (CGI)/Angle on Planet
- Shadowman Vessels
- Quadrant 14
- Narn Jumpgate
- Babylon 5 – Establishing & Transitional (CGI/Composite)
- Sun (CGI/Composite)
- Star With Hand (CGI)
- Jumpgate

TEASER

FADE IN:

1: EXT. SPACE – NEAR CENTAURI PRIME

A CENTAURI WARSHIP passes THROUGH FRAME then we TILT AND PAN DOWN to the planet below. SUPERIMPOSE: Centauri Prime (Homeworld, Centauri Republic). The world is half in eclipse, half out. In the night regions, we should see, even from here, the light of cities along the coastlands in those areas free of clouds. PUSH IN and DISSOLVE THROUGH TO:

2: EXT. CENTAURI CAPITAL

A HIGH SHOT of the city, with art deco-like architecture, somewhere between the round skyscrapers of Buck Rogers and Empire's Cloud City. Green parks and open spaces, a nearby bay. Ostentatious, like all things Centauri. One item in particular catches our eye: a huge PALACE that rises out of the surrounding terrain. We PUSH IN on it.

3: INT. PALACE – GRAND CHAMBER

A pair of double doors OPEN to reveal a CENTAURI PRIME MINISTER. He is in his fifties or sixties, Earth-time, dignified, serious. He enters the huge room, which is spare, but elegant, white drapes hanging from the ceiling and arching across to the walls, where they tumble down along the sides of the walls. PAN AROUND TO REVEAL the dominant feature in the room which is an elevated throne. Like the rest of the room, it is simple but elegant; there is the sense that this throne has been around a long, long time. There's not much else in the place; it's really more of a receiving room than a functional room. FOUR white-veiled Centauri Women stand on either side of the throne, looking down, hands folded. On the throne is the CENTAURI

EMPEROR, in his sixties or seventies, frail but dignified, eyes closed, hands folded in his lap. Most noticeably, he has little or no remaining hair.

The Prime Minister stops in front of the throne. Clears his throat. Nothing. Starts to do so again when:

EMPEROR

I'm not asleep.

And now his eyes open, and there is a small smile on his face. This is a good and gentle man.

PRIME MINISTER

My apologies, majesty. I meant no offense.

EMPEROR

Is everything ready?

PRIME MINISTER

Yes. The royal liner is standing by, and we have adequate warships for protection. They're prepared to set forth as soon as we arrive.

EMPEROR

As soon as *I* arrive. You will remain here.

PRIME MINISTER

I must protest –

EMPEROR

As I expected. But someone must remain here in case there's a crisis, and as my prime minister, you are next in the line of authority.

PRIME MINISTER

I wish you would change your mind. The doctors say your condition is delicate...the least stress –

EMPEROR

All the more reason to go now, while I still can. What remains of our empire stretches before me, and I would see it one more time before I die. What I must do cannot wait any longer.

He rises. The Women on either side move with him. One of them unfolds an ornate hairpiece.

EMPEROR

No need for that. When you get as old as I am, the trappings of status don't mean as much as they used to. I sometimes think that our women are right to shave their heads and rise above such things.

PRIME MINISTER

Majesty –

EMPEROR

I will go among them as I am. There is nothing more to discuss.

He stops, looks around at the room. Smiles, albeit sadly.

EMPEROR

Thank you for taking care of all this again while I sail beyond the sunset one last time. You've given the pilot our first destination?

(Prime Minister nods)

EMPEROR

Good. You've always served me well, old friend, and I think sometimes I do not thank you as much as I should.

(beat)

EMPEROR

Goodbye.

And with a smile, the Emperor moves toward the huge double doors, which part as he approaches. On the face of his Prime Minister, which wells with emotion, suspecting, as we do, that he will never see his emperor again, we go to

4: EXT. BABYLON 5 – ESTABLISHING

JUST A BEAT UNDER:

G'KAR (VO)

This is absolutely intolerable!

5: INT. SHERIDAN'S OFFICE

SHERIDAN sits back, watching with some interest as a pacing, furious G'KAR goes through a display of anger that could take three years off your life just watching it.

G'KAR

This visit by the Centauri Emperor is completely unacceptable to my government! He is a monster, an aberration, a criminal! His family is directly responsible for strip-mining my world! His father personally ordered the execution of a hundred thousand Narns!

SHERIDAN

But he *himself* did nothing, am I correct?

G'KAR

A technicality!

SHERIDAN

In fact, unless I'm mistaken, the current Emperor has gone out of his way to offer your world concessions and return lost territory –

G'KAR

Stolen territory!

SHERIDAN

Whatever. Look, I appreciate the fact that a hundred years of blood isn't something you forget about overnight. But the bottom line is that it's not my problem. This station is open to everyone. If the Emperor wants to visit Babylon 5, I think that's great. It raises our visibility, and helps the folks back home think that maybe we're doing some good.

Sheridan rises, moves toward G'Kar.

G'KAR

So you're going to allow this even over my objections.

SHERIDAN

(looks around)

Did I suddenly turn invisible or something? *Yes*, Ambassador, the Centauri Emperor will be allowed to come aboard. If that bothers you, then I suggest you hide in your quarters, stick your fingers in your ears and hum real loud until it's over. Unless you'd like to try something as breathtakingly rational as trying to open up a dialogue. You're in a position to negotiate directly with the head of the Centauri Republic, and you're wasting it on a tantrum.

He's eye-to-eye with G'Kar. Finally, G'Kar sighs...and there is something fatalistic in his expression.

G'KAR

I shouldn't have expected you to understand, Captain. My mistake. I will not make it again.

G' Kar starts away when:

SHERIDAN

G'Kar...don't do something we'll both regret.

G'KAR

It's too late for that, Captain. Too late by far.

And with that, G'Kar exits, and we

FADE OUT.

END TEASER

ACT ONE

FADE IN:

6: EXT. BABYLON 5

Just a BEAT to establish, then:

7: INT. CUSTOMS AREA

A Human comes through customs, stopping beside one of the CUSTOMS GUARDS, who scans his card. This is a RANGER, one of those whom we've seen in the BG in prior episodes. As the Guard checks his identicard:

CUSTOMS GUARD #1

Back again, eh? That's three times this month.

RANGER

I do a lot of business here.

CUSTOMS GUARD #1

Anything I can help you with?

And then the Ranger looks OS.

8: HIS POV – GARIBALDI

As GARIBALDI moves THROUGH FRAME, talking to someone, although we can't hear him.

9: BACK TO SCENE

As the Ranger takes back his identicard.

RANGER

No, thank you. I've found what I'm looking for.

And with that, the Ranger moves off.

10: INT. LONDO'S QUARTERS

LONDO stands off to one side, listening, as REFA paces the room. VIR sits off to one side, listening with a subtle apprehension.

REFA

– and after the Emperor has made his speech, I've arranged for him to give you an audience. The whole thing will be recorded.

LONDO

Does he know what it's about?

REFA

He believes it's nothing more than a progress report on your situation here. We've taken the liberty of writing your speech for you.

He hands Londo a datacrystal.

REFA

I've had experts in psycholinguistics working on it for weeks. It's perfect; fiery but dignified; elegant, but strong. It outlines the decline of our government and our need for change. It also makes a few predictions about what will go wrong next with the economy, the military...

LONDO

And these predictions, they will come true?

REFA

Already arranged.

Londo exchanges a glance with Vir, who looks down, away, wanting to be anywhere else in the universe but in this room.

LONDO

Sabotage...

REFA

A word or two in the right ear, a critical food shipment delayed... the method is unimportant. All that matters is that when it comes true, the Emperor will look weak and short-sighted, whereas we have our eyes on the future.

Londo considers this, holding the datacrystal out and peering into its faceted depths.

LONDO

You're asking quite a lot of me; after giving this speech, I will not exactly be in favor with the Emperor and his court.

REFA

True...for as long as he's alive. Which shouldn't be much longer. He's never quite recovered from the death of his son, and I'm told his health is fragile at best. When he passes, all that will remain is the memory that we were right. We must position ourselves to move in when the time is right. Image is everything, Mollari. Well, I'll leave you to study the speech. If you have any questions, you know where to find me.

And Refa exits. Londo slowly turns his attention from the datacrystal to Vir.

LONDO

This conversation makes you uncomfortable?

VIR

Yes, it does.

LONDO

Then for once, we have something in common.

(beat)

I am an old man...what is lost by trying? As the Humans say, "Who dares, wins."

VIR

Who dares sometimes gets his head cut off and stuck on a pike.

Londo nods, understanding the stakes here, and closes his hand around the datacrystal, as we go to

11: OMITTED

12: EXT. SPACE – JUMPGATE

As the jumpgate opens, the Centauri liner flashes out, accompanied before and after by three Warship escorts.

13: INT. DOWNBELOW

The Ranger waits. It's a disreputable area, shadowed and isolated. He fits right in. Then we HEAR footsteps. He straightens as a figure in a dark, cowled robe approaches. With a subtle move, a long, thin-bladed knife slides out of his sleeve and into his hand. He doesn't bare it, doesn't make a threatening move, only waits.

The figure stops in front of him. Pulls back the cowl. It's DELENN. The Ranger relaxes slightly at the sight.

DELENN

Did you bring it?

He hands her a datacrystal.

RANGER

The message you were waiting for. I'm to tell you...it's from an old friend.

(beat)

What about the weapons?

DELENN

It is difficult. But I believe I can get you what you need.

14: EXT. BABYLON 5

The Centauri ships are parked alongside Babylon 5, too large to fit inside. A SHUTTLE emerges from the liner and moves toward the docking bay. We FOLLOW IT, then reverse into

15: INT. DOCKING BAY (CGI)

As the shuttle drops down into and through one of the bay doors toward the landing areas elsewhere.

16: INT. CUSTOMS AREA

The place has been cleared of all civilians. Security Guards line the entrances, and stand at attention beside the main door. Sheridan, Garibaldi, Ivanova and FRANKLIN are all there, still in dress uniforms. One of the Guards approaches Garibaldi, whispers to him. Garibaldi nods, and the Guard moves off.

GARIBALDI

(to Sheridan)

He's in. The bay is secure.

SHERIDAN

Initiate Pomp and Circumstance, Commander.

She toggles her link, and the customs area fills with the CENTAURI ANTHEM. As the music plays, there's a BEAT, and then the doors open. The Emperor enters, accompanied by two of the Veiled Women, as before, and a number of Centauri Elite Guards, who wear stylized, almost ancient or traditional looking helmets (not funny big hair helmets, regular looking).

He approaches Sheridan, stops, extends both hands.

EMPEROR

On behalf of the Centauri Republic, I offer the hands of friendship.

SHERIDAN

On behalf of the Earth Alliance, I accept.

They clasp at the forearms and slightly bow, then move apart as Sheridan introduces his staff. (As they're introduced they bow slightly.)

SHERIDAN

This is my second, Commander Susan Ivanova...Chief of Security Michael Garibaldi...and Dr. Stephen Franklin, Chief of Staff of our Medlab facility.

EMPEROR

An honor. News of the work you are doing here has reached even into the Royal Palace on Centauri Prime. I am deeply moved by the knowledge that you would choose to stand in harm's way in the interests of peace.

IVANOVA

Thank you.

SHERIDAN

If you'd like to come this way, we can begin your tour.

EMPEROR

Yes, of course...

They start out, Garibaldi hanging back, eyes all over the place, trusting nothing. The Emperor reaches out and, much to the latter's surprise, touches Franklin's arm.

EMPEROR

Tell me, Doctor, have you seen much of the Vorlon...I believe his name is Kosh?

DR. FRANKLIN

No, no more than anyone else. He's always inside that encounter suit of his. Why?

EMPEROR

I have never seen a Vorlon before, in or out of his shell. Over the centuries we sent many expeditions into Vorlon space. None of them returned. I have heard many strange stories about them...

SHERIDAN

Well, with any luck, Ambassador Kosh will attend the reception along with the other ambassadors.

EMPEROR

But you're not sure...?

SHERIDAN

With Kosh, it's hard to be sure about much of *anything.*

And they head away.

17: INT. G'KAR'S QUARTERS

On the monitor appears another Narn, this one high government. Call him KHA'MAK. G'Kar is in his doublet.

KHA'MAK

The first circle of the Kha'Ri have concluded their deliberations. After much debate, they have endorsed your plan.

G'KAR

Good.

KHA'MAK

G'Quan bless you and hold you in his hands. May he protect you from harm as you do what must be done.

G'KAR

When does the Kha'Ri feel would be the best time?

KHA'MAK

The reception, just before he gives his speech. There will be greater exposure. Are you still prepared to go through with this?

G'KAR

Yes. It is a strange feeling to know, suddenly, that all of the decisions in your life have brought you to this place...that there is no longer doubt, or uncertainty. The future now consists of only three probabilities.

And from a drawer or bureau or box, he removes a clothcovered object...a dagger, carven elaborately in the Narn tradition. He raises it slowly, slowly....

G'KAR

I will stand...and I will turn... and I will strike. In that moment the Emperor and I will both die... or he will die and I will spend my life in prison...or I will fail, and be killed. For the first time in my life, the path is clear...the path is clear.

And the dagger is before his face, and we are CLOSE as we

FADE OUT.

END ACT ONE

ACT TWO

FADE IN:

18: EXT. BABYLON 5 (CGI/COMPOSITE)

PUSHING IN on the Sanctuary window, until we see the Emperor in the window, looking out into space.

19: INT. BABYLON S – BLUE CORRIDOR

Two Centauri Imperial Guards stand on either side of the door as Sheridan approaches with one of the Veiled Centauri Women. The Guards move together, blocking the door.

SHERIDAN

He asked to see me.

They look to the Veiled Woman, who nods. They move apart to permit admission. Sheridan approaches the door, which opens as he enters

20: INT. SANCTUARY

The Emperor stands, alone, looking at the stars, just as we last saw him. Sheridan enters, the door closes behind him.

SHERIDAN

Your majesty.

EMPEROR

Captain.

The Emperor hesitates, and Sheridan can see that there is something else. He approaches, coming up alongside the Emperor and looking out.

EMPEROR

May I ask you a question?

SHERIDAN

Depends on the question, I guess.

EMPEROR

Why are you here...in this place, in that uniform? Was it your choice, or were you pressed into service?

SHERIDAN

It was my choice. The planetary draft didn't start until the War, a few years later. I guess I wanted to serve something that was bigger than I was...maybe even make a difference somewhere, somehow.

(beat)

I was thinking of your comment when you came aboard. You seem very interested in why people chose to be here.

EMPEROR

It has occurred to me recently that I have never chosen anything. I was born into a role that had been prepared for me; I did as I was instructed; married who I was told to marry; took up the role of emperor when my father died; served as husband, father, ruler... I did all I was asked, because it never occurred to me to choose otherwise. And now, at the end of my life...I wonder what might have been.

SHERIDAN

I think we all feel that way, from time to time. That's why my father taught me to live each second as if it were the last moment of my life. He said if you love, love without reservation; if you fight, fight without fear. He called it the way of the warrior.

EMPEROR

No regrets, then?

SHERIDAN

A few...but just a few. You?

EMPEROR

Enough to fill a lifetime.

(points to stars)

There was a time when all this was ours. So much has been lost, so much forgotten... So much blood, so much pain...for what, I wonder? The past tempts us, the present confuses us, the future frightens us...and our lives slip away, moment by moment...lost in the vast, terrible in-between.

(beat)

But there's still time to seize that last, fragile, moment...and choose something better. To make a difference, as you say. And I intend to.

The Emperor turns, and there is a light in his eyes, the look of a man who has seen beyond the edge of his life, to a dream beyond.

EMPEROR

I look forward to seeing you at the reception tonight, Captain. I think you will see something...most extraordinary.

And with that, the Emperor heads away. Sheridan watches him go, then glances back at the stars, as we go to

21: INT. CENTRAL CORRIDOR

As Garibaldi walks with a cluster of other Security Guards.

GARIBALDI

I want this whole section cleared, every entrance and exit checked and re-checked. They'll be coming down any second, and until then, nobody gets in without proper ID. I don't care if you recognize them by sight or not.

And he continues away. As he passes, we PAN ACROSS to a side entrance to the corridor, where we SEE the Ranger, watching, watching...

22: INT. G'KAR'S QUARTERS

G'Kar is speaking to the monitor, which is recording his words (it would be nice if we could see his words appearing on-screen in Narnish as he speaks). He idly touches the dagger atop his desk.

G'KAR

– I take this action without the knowledge or permission of my government. Neither should my aide, Na'Toth, be held accountable for my actions. The responsibility is mine alone. I ask that my remains, and my personal property, be sent back to Narn, to my family. My copy of the Book of G'Quan

I leave to Na'Toth, in the hope of her eventual enlightenment.

He switches off the console. Sits back, closes his eyes.

23: INT. GARDEN/ROTUNDA (CGI)

PUSHING IN on the Rotunda which rises out of the Garden.

24: INT. ROTUNDA

The place is packed with Human VIPs, plus the following: Londo, Delenn, Refa, and in a separate cluster, Franklin, Sheridan, and Ivanova. There is much food and drink.

SHERIDAN

So what's the deal on those veiled Centuari women that follow the emperor around?

IVANOVA

Londo says they're telepaths, raised together since birth. They're linked twenty-four hours a day, no matter how far apart they are. What one sees, the others see. Traditionally, when the emperor leaves, two go with him, and two stay behind.

DR. FRANKLIN

Interesting...it guarantees that he knows what's happening at home, and keeps the royal court up to speed on what he's doing.

IVANOVA

Did the Emperor tell you what this important speech is about?

SHERIDAN

No, he just said it was important. I hoped that might be enough to bring out Ambassador Kosh; looks like I was wrong.

IVANOVA

Too bad, considering what the Emperor said about the Vorlons. He might never get another chance to see one. But I suppose it was too much to hope for.

DR. FRANKLIN

Speaking of too much to hope for... look who just walked in.

They turn, and there is G'Kar, who enters in full diplomatic dress. Sheridan approaches.

SHERIDAN

Ambassador.

G'KAR

Captain.

SHERIDAN

I see you've changed your mind about opening up a dialogue.

G'KAR

I make no promises...but I will hear what he has to say.

SHERIDAN

That's all anyone could ask for.

With that, Sheridan moves away. G'Kar scopes out the room, looks to the raised platform where the Emperor will speak.

25: INT. CREW CORRIDOR

Garibaldi walks PAST CAMERA. A moment later, the Ranger also moves past camera. Following him.

26: AROUND A CORNER

Suddenly Garibaldi grabs the Ranger and shoves him against the wall.

GARIBALDI

Okay, pal, you've got ten seconds to explain why you're following me.

RANGER

I need to talk to you.

GARIBALDI

About what?

The Ranger looks like he's about to answer when two other Guards come on the run.

GARIBALDI

It's okay, I got him.

(to Ranger)

Okay, you said you had to talk to me. About what?

But now the Ranger goes quiet. Looks away.

GARIBALDI

That's what I figured.

(to the guards)

Take him down to holding and keep him there until the reception's over.

He turns the Ranger over to the guards, who nudge him forward, as we go to

27: INT. CENTRAL CORRIDOR

The place has been cleared. The Emperor, his Imperial Guards, and the Veiled Women move into the corridor, heading for the transport tubes at the other end.

28: INT. ROTUNDA – INTERCUT

Laughter, conversation, Londo and Refa off to one side, talking in hushed tones.

29: INT. CENTRAL CORRIDOR – INTERCUT

CLOSE on the Emperor coming into frame. CAMERA SLIGHTLY OVERCRANKED.

30: INT. ROTUNDA – INTERCUT

Delenn approaches G'Kar...but he sees her coming and angles away, his thoughts dark and obsessed.

31: INT. CENTRAL CORRIDOR

The Emperor, surrounded by his entourage, comes closer into frame... CAMERA SLIGHTLY OVERCRANKED ...when he suddenly stops, clutches at his chest. Pain. The wind knocked out of him. His knees weaken. He goes down, clutching at one of the Veiled Women as he falls. One of the Veiled Women screams, all SLOW-SLOW-SLOW as

32: ECU – THE EMPEROR – SLOW MOTION

As his head comes to rest on the floor, unconscious.

33: INT. ROTUNDA

ON Sheridan and Delenn, talking, as Sheridan looks to

34: ANGLE – DR. FRANKLIN

Who gets a call on his link, speaks into it. We see sudden concern on his face, and he sprints for the door.

35: ANGLE – ON SHERIDAN

And from his look, he knows instantly that something is wrong, very wrong. PUSH IN as we GO TO

36: INT. CENTAURI PALACE

The Prime Minister sits on the throne, speaking softly with two Minbari and one Human, when the door opens. In come two of the Veiled Women, heads downcast. The Prime Minister stops dead when he sees them. They approach across the floor, coming to rest on either side of him. He looks from one to the other, and his hand covers his face in grief.

37: EXT. BABYLON 5 – TRANSITIONAL

With the Centauri warships and liner parked outside.

38: INT. MEDLAB

The Emperor is hooked up to a medbed, eyes closed, as Dr. Franklin enters. The two Veiled Women stand behind the bed, eyes downcast. Franklin goes to him, lightly touches his arm.

DR. FRANKLIN

Your majesty...

Slowly the Emperor's eyes open and find Franklin.

DR. FRANKLIN

I wish I'd known of your condition when you arrived. I could've done something... tried something....

(beat)

Your government is asking to have you transferred to your warship, I told them that moving you right now could be fatal. I want your permission to –

The Emperor raises a hand, softly, as if to say, "enough." In his eyes is resignation, he knows he has little time left. When he finally speaks, his voice is a whisper.

EMPEROR

There is something...more important than where I die. A message you must give for me.

DR. FRANKLIN

If it's important, perhaps one of your own people –

EMPEROR

No...if I did, the message might never be delivered. Listen to me, Doctor, listen carefully...

And as Franklin leans in:

39: INT. LONDO'S QUARTERS

Refa paces, Londo and Vir also present.

REFA

This changes everything. We have to move quickly.

LONDO

I agree. I hear word of this has already reached homeworld.

REFA

Our competitors are moving into position, setting themselves up to ascend the throne the moment he dies. Before that happens we have to rise above the others...we must do something extraordinary, something unparalleled...

LONDO

(realization)

He said...just pick a target...

REFA

I'm sorry..?

Londo knows what he has to do...and he also knows the possible massive ramifications of what he is about to say. This must have weight to it. With the following words, the future is forever altered. Vir sees what's coming, like a man watching an accident in slow motion. Londo turns, moves off a bit.

LONDO

I believe there is a Narn colony on the border of Centauri space... Quadrant 14...

VIR

Londo...

REFA

Colony...it's a listening post! They've been using it to spy on us for years! By all rights, that entire planet should be ours!

LONDO

Then let us take it back.

This stops Refa cold. He studies Londo.

REFA

Our military experts have told us the colony is armed to the teeth; we couldn't take it without a major assault... We would lose thousands of lives...

LONDO

I will take care of it. Have your contacts in the military send an expedition to Quadrant 14.

REFA

I can only guarantee a few ships –

LONDO

It will be enough.

REFA

I hope you know what you are doing, Mollari.

And Refa exits. Londo walks away from Vir.

LONDO

Find Mr. Morden. Bring him here.

VIR

Londo...don't do this.

LONDO

I have no choice.

VIR

Yes, you do! Londo, please, I know you don't listen to me, but I'm asking you, this once...don't do this. Once you start down this road there's no going back. You –

LONDO

Do I have to go find him myself?

They're eye to eye. Finally, Vir sighs, shakes his head.

VIR

No...I'll go. I'll go and I'll bring him here. And someday, Londo, I will remind you of this conversation. Maybe...maybe then you'll understand.

And with that Vir exits. When he's gone:

LONDO

(half to himself)

I understand just fine.

(beat)

By this time tomorrow, we will be at war with the Narn. May the Great Maker forgive me....

And on Londo's pained, doomed expression, we

FADE OUT.

END ACT TWO

ACT THREE

FADE IN:

40: EXT. BABYLON 5 – ESTABLISHING

The Centauri warships and liner still parked alongside. PUSH PAST THEM to the station and DISSOLVE THROUGH TO:

41: INT. G'KAR'S QUARTERS

Where G'Kar is practically apoplectic speaking to the wall monitor, on which we SEE the same Narn as before.

G'KAR

I was ready...I had prepared myself ...I had made my peace with the universe, put all my affairs in order... I had the dagger in my hand...and he has the indecency to start dying on his own! Never in my entire life have I seen a case of worse timing! You'd think he could've waited a few more minutes before -

He's interrupted by the doorbell.

G'KAR

Who is it?

DR. FRANKLIN (OS)

Dr. Franklin.

G'KAR

Maybe it's good news...with luck he's feeling better...all they have to do is prop him up for two minutes...I'll call you back. Enter!

G'Kar toggles off. The door opens, and Franklin enters.

DR. FRANKLIN

I just came from seeing the Centauri Emperor.

G'KAR

How is the poor fellow? I was so looking forward to meeting him and opening up a dialogue.

DR. FRANKLIN

Funny, he was looking forward to meeting you, too. He had a message for you. Given his present condition, he's asked me to relay that message for him.

G'KAR

I have no time for threats -

DR. FRANKLIN

He wanted to say that he's sorry.

And this is the last thing G'Kar ever expected to hear. You could knock him over with a feather.

G'KAR

What?

DR. FRANKLIN

He came all the way out here, risked his health, endangered his life, so he could stand beside a Narn, in neutral territory, and apologize...for all the things the Centauri have done to your people, for all the things his family did. He said, "We were wrong. We knew we were wrong when we were there and when we left, but we never said it. The hatred between our people can never end until someone is willing to say, 'I'm sorry,' and try to find a way to make it right again, to atone for our actions."

G'Kar sits heavily, astonished.

DR. FRANKLIN

He said it was the only choice he'd ever made in his life...and now that seems to have been taken away from him.

G'KAR

I had...I had no idea...

DR. FRANKLIN

No, I'm sure you didn't...and maybe that's the biggest tragedy in the whole damned story.

(beat)

Good night, Ambassador.

And with that, Franklin exits, leaving behind a stunned and shattered G'Kar.

42: EXT. BABYLON 5 – TRANSITIONAL

The station moves into eclipse, the sun fading.

43: INT. LONDO'S QUARTERS

Londo sits, asleep, a drink in his hand. PUSH IN on him, and DISSOLVE INTO:

44: START DREAM MONTAGE

The destruction of the monitoring station at Raghesh 3.

Londo in the council chambers from "Chrysalis."

LONDO

Keep this up, Ambassador, and soon you won't have a planet to protect.

45: EXT. SUN (CGI)

A red sun burns hot...and from the sun comes the specter of a dark hand, thousands of miles across, flames licking the edges, seeming to turn slightly and grasp. (DO NOT USE A CGI CONSTRUCT FOR THE HAND, ROTOSCOPE A REAL HAND.)

46: EXT. CENTAURI PRIME

A quick shot, then:

47: DOWNSHOT – LONDO

Standing in the open air as he shields his eyes, looks up to the sky.

48: UPSHOT – THE SKY

As a squadron of full-scale Shadowmen vessels fly overhead.

49: INT. CENTAURI PALACE – GRAND CHAMBER

CLOSE on Londo as he bows to receive a simple crown, a loop of metal with a single gem in the front, over the forehead. The room is white, bright. Londo looks up

50: REVERSE

The same palace room is dark, splotches of red and black lighting, shadowed, the tapestries and veils torn, hanging.

51: ON LONDO

As he looks around...and he is a much older Londo, sitting on the throne, tired, his hair streaked with grey, a pallor in his face.

52: HIS POV – A DARK WALL

And we see slitted EYES seemingly peering out of nowhere in the darkness.

53: BACK ON LONDO

As he looks forward again.

54: REVERSE

G'Kar stands before Londo. G'Kar is older, and one eye is covered with a patch, his face marked by a scar.

55: EXT. STAR WITH HAND (CGI)

As the hand reaches fully out until it nearly touches us.

56: CLOSE – LONDO AND G'KAR

Their hands wrapped around one another's throats, face to face, on the floor, strangling the life out of one another.

57: INT. LONDO'S QUARTERS – END OF DREAM MONTAGE

Londo awakes with a start, looks around.

LONDO

The time...what is the time...?

He grabs a small clock, looks at it.

LONDO

It's begun.

Mollari rises, heads OS.

58: EXT. SPACE – PLANETSIDE

A Narn cruiser is silhouetted against the planet, with a number of other Narn ships and an orbiting Narn base nearby. Superimpose: Narn Colony. Quadrant 14.

59: ANOTHER ANGLE (CGI)

As three Shadowmen vessels PHASE INTO VIEW...and they come in FIRING.

60: ON THE STATION

As it's hit, ships zipping out of the way of the debris like bees.

61: THE BATTLE

A Ron Thorton special. Absolute carnage, worse by far than the assault on Quadrant 37.

61A-C: INT. NARN FIGHTER

The NARN PILOT #1 REACTS to the OS BURST of light from the explosion.

NARN PILOT #1

By G'Lan....

(beat)

Break away! Break off!

(beat)

Attack! All wings, attack!

(beat)

Keep them away from the colony! Can't let them get past us!

(beat)

Shrock, no...where are they coming from? What are they?!

Then, with almost all of his forces gone, he gives a long YELL, as his ship FIRES at the incoming Shadow vessels... and we PUSH IN on his yell as red-blue LIGHT fills the screen, and his ship is destroyed.

62: EXT. NARN CITY (CGI)

Three-quarters shot, high angle. We only SEE the Narn city for a moment as a beam suddenly arcs in from space and BLASTS it.

63: EXT. ANGLE ON PLANET

And where the beam struck, the planet ERUPTS in a blast that is similar in appearance to the volcanoes on Io: seen in silhouette, a geyser against space.

64: EXT. SPACE – SHADOWMEN VESSELS

As they finish blowing the last Narn ships to hell...and PHASE out of view.

65: INT. BABYLON 5 – ZOCALO

Londo walks with Refa, their voices low.

REFA

You're sure it's done?

LONDO

Yes. The Narns should be hearing about it soon. Our forces can move in at any time.

REFA

Then I'll have to move quickly. There's still one more thing I have to take care of back home...an obstacle to remove.

LONDO

What's that?

REFA

Better you don't know.

Refa heads quickly off. Londo, tired, starts to turn away when he HEARS:

G'KAR (OS)

Mollari!

He turns to see G'Kar lumbering after him. Fearing the worst, Londo picks up his pace, heads for the transport tubes. The door closes before he can get to it, and G'Kar catches up to him.

G'KAR

You!

LONDO

I can explain everything –

G'KAR

I am going to buy you...a drink!

And he practically drags Londo to the bar, sits him down.

LONDO

I don't – I'm not sure I –

During the following, as what this is about dawns on Londo, his torment and discomfort grows exponentially.

G'KAR

Sit, Mollari. It's not everyday I get a revelation, you know. I've heard something that makes me think there may be hope for us after all. I'd believed your people capable of only murder and pain. But apparently there is still a spark of decency in your genetic code. It's not much of a foundation, I'll grant you that, but it's a start.

A pair of drinks are delivered. G'Kar takes one, hands the other to Londo.

G'KAR

I never thought I would be saying this, Mollari, but...to the health of your Emperor...and, perhaps, to your health as well.

He clicks Londo's glass. Londo is in terrible psychological pain, knowing what G'Kar doesn't know about what's coming.

LONDO

To the Emperor.

(beat)

Thank you.

They drink. Londo wishes he were at the bottom of a deep hole.

66: EXT. QUADRANT

As several Centauri warships come out of jump, surrounded by a flurry of fighters.

WIDEN AS they move through a cloud of debris...ruined Narn fighters, cruisers, absolute carnage.

67: EXT. NARN JUMPGATE

As it FLASHES, and out comes a dozen or so Narn fighters. They must emerge in a different direction than the Centauri cruisers, so they don't see them at first.

NARN FIGHTER (VO)
We've lost the distress signal.

68: INT. NARN FIGHTER

NARN FIGHTER #2 sits at the controls...devastated by what he sees.

NARN FIGHTER #2
No...destroyed...all of it gone.... Who could have done this? Who –

NARN FIGHTER (VO)
Centauri warships detected! Closing fast!

NARN FIGHTER #2
Centauri!? Alert homeworld! Prepare to attack!

NARN FIGHTER (VO)
Sir, we're outnumbered! We don't have a chance!

NARN FIGHTER #2
Then we die with honor!

69: EXT. SPACE

As the Narn fighters swing around, and begin heading toward the vastly overwhelming Centauri forces. They haven't got a chance in hell.

70: INT. CENTAURI PALACE – GRAND CHAMBER

The Prime Minister walks the room, touches the throne, his thoughts far away, concerned. Suddenly the room is plunged into darkness. He wheels around.

71: HIS POV

Three or four Centauri stand silhouetted against the light of the doorway behind them. We can see only their shapes.

PRIME MINISTER (OS)

Who is it? Who's there?

As one, they begin to move forward.

72: REVERSE – ON THE PRIME MINISTER

Backing away, but nowhere to go, as their shadows fall across him.

PRIME MINISTER

Guards! Guards!

73: CLOSE ANGLE

As a knife pierces the Prime Minister's ribs. PAN UP QUICKLY to where his eyes are wide in pain...and yet somehow sad...as he slowly slides OUT OF FRAME.

74: LOW ANGLE SHOT

Shooting past the motionless Prime Minister, on the floor, to where the Silhouetted Figures move out of the room, their work completed.

75: INT. GARIBALDI'S OFFICE

A tired Garibaldi rubs his eyes as ZACK ALLAN enters.

ZACK ALLAN

The prisoner is asking to speak to you again.

GARIBALDI

C'mon...give me a break, you know the kind of day it's been.

ZACK ALLAN

He says it's important.

GARIBALDI

Okay...okay, fine, send him in.

Zack retreats OS. A moment later, the Ranger enters.

GARIBALDI

All right, you've got five minutes.

RANGER

I was sent to find you. I have a message.

He reaches toward a sleeve, and peels back a layer in which a datacrystal has been concealed. He holds it out to Garibaldi, puts it on the console.

RANGER

I believe it will explain everything.

Garibaldi hesitates for a moment, then picks up the crystal. Inserts it into a port.

GARIBALDI

Play.

A beat ... and on the monitor there suddenly appears the face of JEFFREY SINCLAIR.

SINCLAIR

Hello, old friend. It's been a while.

And on Garibaldi's stunned expression, we

FADE OUT.

END ACT THREE

ACT FOUR

FADE IN:

76: INT. GARIBALDI'S OFFICE

As before. A stunned Garibaldi looks at the screen, on which we SEE Sinclair.

SINCLAIR

My job on the Minbari homeworld is more than just representing Earth. The President doesn't know about that part yet...and I don't think it'd be wise for you to tell him. There's a great darkness coming, Michael. Some of the Minbari have been waiting for it a long time. Preparing for it. Others ... don't believe it. They still think we're the enemy. We're not. And we have to get past that, or the darkness will overwhelm us all. So we're taking steps to change that.

77: INT. OBSERVATION DOME

As Ivanova approaches Sheridan, her face grave.

IVANOVA

Captain...we just intercepted a message from the Narn Homeworld to Ambassador G'Kar.

SHERIDAN

I thought we didn't eavesdrop on our ambassadors.

IVANOVA

We don't. This was an open channel. I think

they wanted us to hear it. The Centauri have launched a full-scale assault on a Narn colony in Quadrant 14.

SHERIDAN

Damn....

78: INT. GARIBALDI'S OFFICE

As before. The message continues.

SINCLAIR

The bearer of this message is one of my Rangers.

79: ANGLE ON THE RANGER

Impassive, unmoved, listening

SINCLAIR (OS)

Some are Minbari, most are Humans. They've been drawn here to learn to work together, and prepare for the fight ahead.

80: BACK TO SCENE

As Garibaldi freezes the image.

GARIBALDI

That's right...when I saw you, I kept thinking I'd seen you before, but it wasn't you...just some others who were dressed pretty much the same.

RANGER

We've been here for almost two months, Mr. Garibaldi...keeping an eye on things. We are an army, small but growing.

GARIBALDI

An army needs weapons. Are they coming through here?

RANGER

No, but we do have friends here. That's all I can say for now.

Garibaldi glances back at the monitor, unfreezes the image.

SINCLAIR

Their job for now is to patrol the frontier, to listen, to watch...and return with reports too sensitive to entrust to regular channels. That means they'll be coming through Babylon 5 on a regular basis. They are my eyes and ears; where you see them, you see me.

81: INT. G'KAR'S QUARTERS

With G'Kar on the line with Kha'Mak.

KHA'MAK

The first reports from Quadrant 14 were confused. They weren't sure who was attacking them. But the returning fighters confirmed that Centauri warships were leading the assault.

G'KAR

What about our people? There were over a quarter million of us there.

KHA'MAK

There were...heavy casualties. Most of those killed died in the first few minutes of the assault. As for the survivors...you know how the Centauri are. Now that they've taken control, I doubt we'll see any of them again.

(beat)

I don't understand how they could have wiped out our defenses so quickly...I just don't understand it. I'll report more when I learn it.

And Kha'Mak blips off the screen. G'Kar turns...and in his eyes is a rage that is terrible to behold.

G'KAR

...I reached out my hand...and he betrayed me...*he knew and he betrayed me!*

And he begins tearing up the place, throwing anything not tied down, a HOWL of RAGE bellowing from somewhere deep inside.

82: INT. GARIBALDI'S OFFICE

As the message concludes:

SINCLAIR

In the name of our friendship, I ask that you give them every courtesy and cooperation. I...I wish I could tell you more, wish I could warn you...but the others don't think it's time yet.

(beat)

I hope to see you again soon, old friend. Until then, take care. Stay close to the Vorlon. And watch out for shadows. They move when you're not looking at them.

And the image BLIPS off. Garibaldi sits back.

GARIBALDI

Well, I'll be a son of a –

Just then the console BEEPS at him. Coming out of it, he toggles it.

GARIBALDI

Yeah..?

ZACK ALLAN (VO)

We've got a yellow alert in the ambassadorial wing! We need help, fast! It's G'Kar

His voice is cut off.

GARIBALDI

Zack...Zack...

(toggle link)

Station house to all security in Green Sector, yellow alert!

83: INT. GREEN SECTOR HALLWAY

Just as G'Kar picks up a Security Guard and THROWS him the length of the hall and backhands two others. This hulking, lethal force of nature is the Narn who fought against the Centauri before...enraged and feral, crouched and looking for blood. He stalks ahead.

G'KAR

Mollari...MOLLARI!

He rounds a corner, and finds a line of armed Security Guards, PPGs aimed and ready, and Sheridan standing in front of them. (Sheridan is not armed.)

SHERIDAN

That's far enough.

G'KAR

Mollari!

SHERIDAN

Go back to your quarters and no charges will be pressed.

G'Kar starts a step forward. The PPGs come up, aiming at him.

SHERIDAN

I mean it, G'Kar. You will go back to your quarters and you will go back now.

G'Kar is in bloodlust mode...he speaks, but it's an effort. Sheridan slowly approaches.

G'KAR

They're doing it to us...doing it to us again...I won't let this happen...I won't let it happen again!

SHERIDAN:

Then you're going to need all the help you can get, and you can't do that if you're not here. Set one foot in Ambassador Mollari's quarters and you'll either be dead or gone. Either way it won't help your people.

G'KAR

They'll kill everyone! Don't you understand? They've done it before! They'll kill everyone...

SHERIDAN

Then you have to decide what's more important to you, G'Kar...revenge, or saving the lives of your people?

He's now eye to eye with G'Kar. For a moment it looks like this could go either way. Then G'Kar breaks eye contact... steps away toward a wall, touches it, leans against it...and slides down, to the floor, hands covering head, overwhelmed and torn by his emotions. One of the Guards starts to come toward him, but Sheridan waves him off, feeling G'Kar's anguish.

SHERIDAN

No...leave him alone. Leave him alone.

We LINGER for just a moment...on G'Kar...then go to

84: INT. MEDLAB

The Emperor, looking very much on his last legs, barely manages to open an eye as Dr. Franklin runs a scanner over him, checking his signs. He opens his mouth, works to say something. Nothing quite comes out.

DR. FRANKLIN

It's okay...easy...you should try to save your strength. Is there anything you want?

EMPEROR

(softly, barely)

I would very much...like to have seen...a Vorlon...

Dr. Franklin nods, touches his arm gently, moves off. MOVE IN CLOSE on the Emperor, give it a BEAT... and a shadow falls over him. He looks up.

85: HIS POV – KOSH

Looms over him.

86: BACK TO SCENE

As the Emperor reaches forth a hand to him.

EMPEROR

How will...this end?

KOSH

In fire.

87: INT. SHERIDAN'S OFFICE

Ivanova, Sheridan, and Garibaldi are gathered.

IVANOVA

What makes you think you can trust this source of yours?

GARIBALDI

Let's just say he comes highly recommended.

SHERIDAN

You're holding something back.

GARIBALDI

Yes, sir.

SHERIDAN

Why?

GARIBALDI

I gave my word.

SHERIDAN

Garibaldi...you're asking me to accept sensitive information without any idea where it comes from.

(beat)

I could order you to tell me.

GARIBALDI

And if I told you, you'd never be able to trust me with anything confidential, knowing that someone above you could order me to talk.

It's a good point. Sheridan finally sighs, relents.

SHERIDAN

All right. Go on.

GARIBALDI

Ever since New Year's, we've been hearing about some other major race on the prowl. My source tells me the rumors are true...and there may be some link to the Centauri Government. Who or what that link is, I don't know. But they're definitely getting support.

IVANOVA

And you think this other race was behind the assault on Quadrant 14?

GARIBALDI

It's possible.

SHERIDAN

If it's true...they won't want that information to get out.

IVANOVA

What information? All we have here is supposition.

SHERIDAN

Sheridan's Rule number 29: always make your opponent think you know more than you really know.

(beat)

If your source is right, we may be able to play a bluff.

88: INT. MEDLAB

Refa, Londo, the Veiled Women, Dr. Franklin, and the Imperial Guard are gathered around the Emperor's bed. He doesn't have far to go.

DR. FRANKLIN

I repeat: This is completely inappropriate; he's in no condition to –

REFA

He is the Emperor...and the good of our people comes first. If he could, he would tell you so himself. This cannot wait.

REFA

(to Emperor)

Your Majesty....

Slowly, the Emperor slits open his eyes.

REFA

Majesty...we have wonderful news. We have retaken the Narn colony in Quadrant 14. It fell within a matter of hours, and not one of our people was hurt or killed in the process. All of Homeworld is rejoicing... we are again what we should be. All we lack is your blessing.

The Emperor tries to speak, but nothing comes, barely a whisper. Refa lowers his head, to listen, but with a frail hand, the Emperor nudges him away. Looks to Londo, on the other side.

Londo lowers his head, his ear barely an inch from the Emperor's lips. A few words emerge...then he simply stops. Londo rises, slowly. Looks to Dr. Franklin, who runs a scanner over him.

DR. FRANKLIN

He's dead.

Refa looks to Londo.

REFA

What did he say?

LONDO

He said...continue...take my people back...to the stars.

The two Veiled Women exchange a glance, and exit.

89: INT. HALLWAY BETWEEN INFIRMARY/MEDLAB

The Veiled Women exit, followed a moment later by Londo and Refa. They wait until they're more or less alone, then:

REFA

Mollari...what did he say...really?

LONDO

He said...that we are both damned.

REFA

(considers)

Well...it's a small enough price to pay...for immortality.

And with that, Refa walks away.

90: INT. G'KAR'S QUARTERS

G'Kar sits in the darkness as the door opens, and Sheridan enters. He approaches the motionless G'Kar.

SHERIDAN

Ambassador.

(nothing)

We think we have an idea how we can help. I've called a council meeting. I hope

you'll come. I think it's important that you
be there.

No reply from G'Kar. Sheridan starts out, when he turns at:

G'KAR

Sheridan.
(beat)
I will attend.
(beat)
Thank you...for stopping me.

Sheridan nods, and exits. As G'Kar closes his eyes, go to

91: EXT. BABYLON 5

A transitional shot, to get us into

92: INT. COUNCIL CHAMBERS

Present: Londo, Delenn, Sheridan, Kosh. No G'Kar.

SHERIDAN

Ambassador Mollari...what about the Narn civilian population? I'm told there are over a quarter million of them at the colony. Will you let them return to the Narn homeworld?

LONDO

I'm afraid we can't do that. But I'm sure my government will find some productive activity for them.

DELENN

Forced labor camps...

Just then, they turn. G'Kar stands silently in the door. Even Londo can't bring himself to meet G'Kar's gaze. Slowly, with dignity, G'Kar moves to his seat on the Council.

LONDO

(awkward now)

Simple retraining. We have no desire to misuse anyone.

SHERIDAN

Ambassador. Would you like to make an opening statement?

G'Kar shakes his head. No. Sheridan looks to Londo.

SHERIDAN

I should mention that I've just received permission from my government to send observers to the colony. Their job will be to monitor the treatment of the Narn civilian population.

LONDO

They're not welcome.

SHERIDAN

Well, we're sending them anyway. Unless you'd like to try shooting down an Earthforce transport...and personally, I'd advise against it. My people aren't looking for another war...but they don't take kindly to being shot at.

(beat)

Our observers will assess the situation, interview the survivors, and put together a full report... including as much as they can find out about just how the colony was conquered so quickly. I think we'd all be interested to know how you did this, Ambassador.... And trust me, if our observers go there, they *will* find out.

The latter is a definite warning to Londo, and its meaning is not lost. Londo considers, then:

LONDO

I believe...I believe I may be able to convince my government to allow the colony's civilian population to leave the area, and return safely to the Narn home-world as a gesture of good will. This would remove the need for observers from Earth, wouldn't you agree, Captain?

SHERIDAN

Under those conditions...yes. I'm sure your...goodwill effort will be appreciated for what it is, Ambassador.

Londo smiles.

Sheridan smiles back. Both knowing the high stakes game they're playing.

DELENN

The Minbari Government is willing to provide transportation for the Narn, if that is agreeable to both parties.

LONDO

Absolutely.

DELENN

(to G'Kar)

Ambassador G'Kar?

G'Kar nods. He's got something on his mind.

SHERIDAN

Is there something else?

G'KAR

(nods)

Before coming here, I received a communique from my government. For a hundred years, the Centauri occupied our world, devastated it. We swore we would never let that happen again. This attack against our largest civilian colony has inflicted terrible damage and loss of life. They have crossed a line we cannot allow them to cross. As a result...two hours ago my government officially declared war against the Centauri Republic.

(beat)

Our hope for peace is over. We are now at war...we are now at war.

And on the stunned expression of the Council members, we

FADE OUT.

END ACT FOUR

TAG

FADE IN:

93: EXT. BABYLON 5 – ESTABLISHING

As the Centauri warship and liner move away from the station.

94: INT. OBSERVATION DOME

Ivanova is at her post as Sheridan enters.

IVANOVA

Centauri vessels are heading for the jump-gate...taking the Emperor home.

SHERIDAN

Godspeed.

IVANOVA

Did you notify Earth Central about the declaration of war?

SHERIDAN

(nods)

They're obviously concerned, but they know it takes time to build up a full-scale interstellar war; both sides have to assign ships, develop strategies, create supply lines... I figure we'll have some border skirmishes for the next few months before it builds to total war. With luck, we can negotiate this out before it reaches that stage.

IVANOVA

I don't know... This time the Centauri have outside help, and for all we know, they could be ready for total war now.

SHERIDAN

Leave it to you to find the black cloud behind every silver lining, Commander.

IVANOVA

That's my job, sir.

95: EXT. JUMPGATE

As the Centauri ships depart.

96: INT. LONDO'S QUARTERS

Refa, Londo and Vir are present.

REFA

– and the unfortunate death of the Prime Minister, so soon after the Emperor, has had the effect of tilting the balance of power back home. Several competing families have been neutralized, leaving the Emperor's nephew to claim the throne...a young man who feels as we do about the future.

LONDO

And the declaration of war?

Refa moves toward the door.

REFA

This threat has only put our new Emperor more squarely on our side. If the Narns want a war, we will give it to them. And then some.

(beat)

For the first time in a hundred years, Ambassador, our people are on the right track again. And we have you to thank for it. You will find the new Emperor's gratitude most...rewarding. Good day, Mollari.

Refa exits. As the door closes, Londo turns to find Vir's eyes on him.

VIR

I'm surprised...you could've asked to be named to the royal court. It would've put you in the position to become emperor yourself someday. That is what you want, isn't it?

97: FLASHBACK REPRISE

QUICK CUTS: As Londo is crowned...is old...and at the last of his life, is locked in mortal combat with G'Kar.

98: BACK TO SCENE

As Londo shakes off the memory.

LONDO

No...I have no desire to be emperor. A coronation is nothing more than a sign to assassins that a new target has been set up on the firing range. I prefer to work from behind the scenes.... The reward is nearly as great, and the risk far, far less.

And Londo moves past Vir, who looks very dubious about this entire enterprise.

99: INT. CUSTOMS AREA

As Garibaldi walks the Ranger toward customs.

GARIBALDI

– so I want to thank you again for your help. You may have saved the lives of a quarter-million Narns.

RANGER

Then you will give us the cooperation we need?

GARIBALDI

On one condition. I want you to keep me informed on what you and the other Rangers hear out there. We've got a shooting war on our hands, and we can use all the information we can get.

RANGER

Consider it done...if you keep our presence here a secret.

GARIBALDI

You got a deal.

(The Ranger starts off.)

GARIBALDI

Oh...one last thing. Aside from me, does anybody *else* know you're here?

RANGER

Just one other.

And the Ranger heads away.

100: INT. DELENN'S QUARTERS

As she enters a datacrystal into the viewer. Sinclair's face appears on the monitor.

SINCLAIR

Hello, old friend.

And we PUSH IN on her face, as we

FADE OUT.

THE END